Plague Wolf

PARKER JACK PLUMER

Trashcan Printing

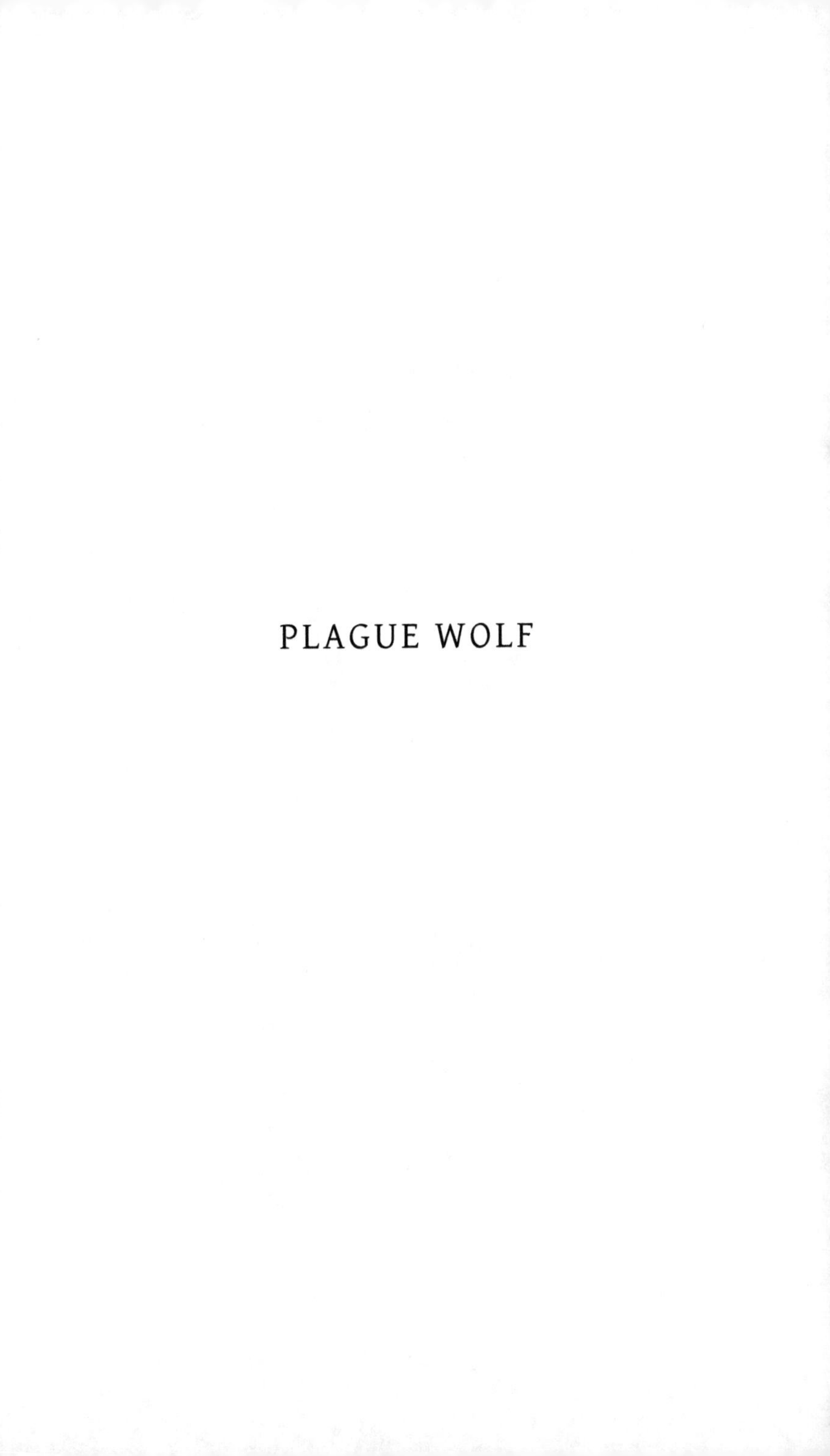

PLAGUE WOLF

Dedication

"You've probably written enough words to have written at least 3 novels by now." - My husband answered when I asked if I should try to write a novella. So this one is dedicated to him. My most perfect Scoundrel.

CONTENTS

INTRODUCTION

Redemption. The act of atoning for a fault or mistake. The deliverance from sins humanity carries with them through this mortal coil. The repurchase of something sold. The extent to which a man seeks redemption speaks to his nature. Some sins cannot be forgiven, and transgressions that can never be forgotten. Can the light of heaven shine upon a soul blackened by the truest of evil? A shadowy figure walks reckless and forgotten paths in search of this answer. The passage of time plays no part in his quest. Only the eternal determination of absolution will finish his story and reveal his destiny.

CHAPTER ONE

~ I ~

SNOWFALL

A plume of wet breath momentarily heated the red, prickly flesh that peeked through the wool wrapped around Oliver's face. Flecks of snowflakes dusted part of his coat and hat. His rifle lay on his lap, loaded and ready for use on the first deer or prey passing by. Hunting had never been one of his strong suits, and honestly, the idea of killing any living creature made his stomach churn.

His father had always been tough on him because of his sensitivity, but his mother had encouraged it. Not enough men in the world were keen and willing to show kindness. Oliver's father passed away several years ago. The doctors had determined that his death was caused by brain injury or cholera. Oliver knew better. His father couldn't handle even a single glass of whiskey, let alone the copious amounts he tended to drink. The doctors had said before that if he didn't stop, it would be the death of him. They had been right.

The snap of a twig sounded through the snowfall. The broken silence brought Oliver back to the present. He straightened up in his seated position and grabbed his rifle, ready to aim. His bright blue eyes widened as Oliver looked around for the source of the noise. The white blanket on the ground and the trees made spotting the deer's brown hide easier. There were three of them, but they were too far away to shoot, so he waited till they came closer.

Brown and evergreen branches bent and swayed under the piling snow. It was affecting the visibility of the deer. Oliver readied a shot, or he'd lose his chance altogether. Thank God one deer, a doe, had gotten close enough for him to take a chance. He raised his repeater, peered down the barrel, and aimed the site squarely at the doe. Oliver took a deep breath, held it, and squeezed the trigger. A whip-like crack followed by the sonic boom of the shot echoed off of the rocks surrounding him. Oliver lowered his weapon to see two deer take off while one fell to the ground with a bleat of fear and pain. He rose from his position with a growl while his joints protested stiffness and cold. As he headed toward the downed creature, a snow cloud blew off him. The bullet's path was true to its mark, making the deer's death swift and merciful. The next part of field-dressing he was more comfortable with. The growing city needed this food, and being a doctor, he was not squeamish against blood and gore. Only the taking of life that bothered him about hunting, despite it needing to be done.

Once he finished, Oliver hefted the doe onto his shoulder and made the trek back to where he'd hitched his horse. Snowfall covered the coat of the brown mare. The doe's body was tied behind his saddle, and the rifle stowed; Oliver mounted up and headed toward the meeting point he and the five other hunters had chosen. On the way there, the wind whipped the light snow into little frenzies of swirls. The colder he became, his nose ran faster until he feared icicles might form off the tip. The weather was problematic since the group was a respectful distance from home. If things kept getting worse, they could not descend the mountains safely.

Oliver pulled his coat and hat around him as much as possible. He wasn't far from the meeting point when he felt eyes on him. What if a predator had tracked the smell of his kill? A shiver shook his body that was not fully due to the cold, and he prayed that was not the case. However, the thought that someone was watching him made him just as nervous. The sun was setting faster than Oliver expected, and the snowfall made it even darker. He turned around a large boulder that was a landmark before the meeting spot. A sharp whistle cut through the strong wind, which Oliver recognized and returned. Moments later, he and two of the other hunters had gathered. Ten minutes later, the other three hunters joined them. Three of them had also been successful in making a kill.

"Daniel, is that your blood or your kill's blood?" Oliver asked as he moved his mare closer to him. A stream of fresh blood ran down the older man's hand and dripped onto the snow.

"My own. Damned wolf must have been tracking the same elk I was. One moment, I was preparing to shoot and the next, this black devil was coming after me," he explained. The wolf was thrown over the back of his horse. "I was lucky I could shoot with my pistol, but not before he bit my forearm. Obviously, the elk ran, but I figured I might as well bring the wolf. A good black wolf's skin could fetch a good price," Daniel said. Chapped lips curled into a proud smile and etched deeper the lines around his eyes. Daniel had lived in these mountains all his life, and his knowledge was priceless. No one actually knew how old he was. His hair and beard were gray, but the mountaineer did not particularly resemble a man over fifty years old. He also enjoyed being mysterious and would laugh whenever asked about his past.

Oliver reached over to gently take hold of the injured arm to see the damage. "We'll get that fixed up as soon as we can, alright? Until then, try to keep the wound held up to slow the bleeding," he said. While the wound was still bleeding, it wasn't enough that he felt he needed to do a tourniquet on it. "Jake, what are we going to do? The snow is getting worse, and the wind is turning fierce. Think we can make it back tonight?" Oliver asked. Jake was the leader of the hunting party. In his forties, the stout man's presence was akin to a grizzly bear among black bears, and he was used to being in charge. He was also relatively silent and remained silent as he mulled over the options.

"Do we have any other choice? This storm could twist into a blizzard, and we haven't prepared for a long stay out in the wilderness," Emmanuel stated with concern. He was younger, barely in his twenties, and quite green at everything that didn't involve mining for gold. His baby face, wrapped in long greasy brown hair, looked at Jake with more fear than the others felt. Jake had not wanted to bring him with them on this hunt, but eventually, Emmanuel's mother convinced him to take the kid along.

"Calm yourself, Manny. Things aren't as dire as they seem to be," Horace's deep, grating voice broke through the wind. He was an older miner, but instead of gray hair, his hair was still a stark black. His smallpox face looked hard and mean, but past that exterior was a sweet man. He had been the one to help Oliver understand that killing for food was not the evil he felt it to be. An aura of melancholy seemed to travel with him everywhere. It had been that way since his wife had passed away.

"I know of a cabin close to here, Jake. It was abandoned the last time I checked. If it is still standing, it should make an adequate shelter for us until this storm passes over," Daniel said. This information caused a cacophony of complaints and a chaotic chorus of opinions on whether they should try to head back or go to the cabin.

"Quiet, the lot of you," Jake ordered, waiting until the buzz died before he spoke again. "We'll head for the cabin. If this weather continues, rather not try to get the horses down in the dark. Daniel, can you lead us there?"

"That I can, boss," with the assurance given, he led them toward the promised shelter. It wasn't long before they knew that Jake had made the right decision as the snowstorm worsened. Everyone filed in line and settled into their saddles for the trek to the cottage, where they could find warmth. By the time they reached the cabin, the sun's last rays were dying, and a veil of white covered the world. Thank the good Lord that the place was still standing, as was the small stable where they could keep the horses.

"Clyde and Horace, you two find a safe place to store the kills. It looks like there is a small shed near the stable that would work. Emmanuel and Oliver take care of the horses. Daniel, you're with me. Let's check out the inside of the cabin and get a fire started for our cold bones," Jake gave out orders as they all dismounted.

Oliver went with Clyde and Horace to get the kills off the horses and then led them to the stable, where Emmanuel took the tack off the other three horses. "Do you think we'll get trapped up here, Doc?" the young man asked.

"No, I don't think so. I think we'll be able to leave tomorrow. Even if we can't, we're in good shape to ride nature out. Don't worry, Manny. We'll be fine," Oliver said confidently as he gave the young man a pat on the shoulder and a smile. He hoped he was right, but Mother Nature could be fickle up in the mountains. If you didn't respect her, it would easily be your last. "Go on in and get warm, Manny. I'll take care of the last horse," he offered kindly. They were all frozen, but Manny was just a kid, and Oliver was the kind of guy that put everyone else first. The lad gave his thanks before he left the stable and headed to the cabin, where it was warmer.

"There we go, guys. All nice and warm," Oliver whispered as he patted his mare on the rump. He'd come out later to provide them with water, but first, he'd have to melt some snow. Oliver grabbed his hat and left the stable, shutting the door behind him. Then he felt as if he were being watched again. The doctor turned and looked into the woods, covered by darkness, to see if he could find the source of his discomfort. In the direction from which they came, red eyes looked upon him. A shiver went down his spine in a wave of fear. He never took his eyes off them or even blinked, but they suddenly vanished. Oliver wasted no more time heading into the cabin with the others.

The difference in temperature from outside to inside the cozy cabin was pleasant. A fire was already crackling, and some compassionate soul had already started brewing coffee. Oliver hung his hat and stripped it from his heavy winter coat to hang it with the others. He was an average-built man in his late twenties, who stood on the taller side at six feet even, and his hair was short but messy and dirty-blond. The dimples in his cheeks were so deep that not even the five o'clock shadow could hide them. He moved to stand before the fire to warm his hands up before working on Daniel's arm. Despite the wind blowing hard, it wasn't seeping through cracks around the windows or walls. A table seating four was in front of the fireplace. A stove and pantries were in one corner. Two rocking chairs and a tall bookshelf sat in the other. There seemed to be a bedroom in a separate room and a tiny storage closet.

"Okay, Daniel. Let me dress that wound up for you," Oliver said as he got his compact doctor's bag and moved over to the table. He opened it, took Daniel's arm, and gently rolled up the tattered and bloodied sleeve. There were a few deep puncture wounds on the top and bottom of his arm, no doubt from where the wolf had bitten down on him. "This isn't too bad. You got lucky, old man. A wolf that size could have done much more damage," Oliver teased the man as he cleaned the wound. He was careful, but Daniel still winced in pain.

"Damned bastard. That son of a bitch almost got me by the neck," Daniel said with some morbid amusement. He fell silent then; a somewhat disturbing look crossed his weathered face. "To be honest, I'm surprised it didn't. It was as if he only cared about chewing on me a little. I had just gotten my pistol out to shoot him, but I don't think he would've let me go before that. I tell ya, Ollie, there was something wrong with that wolf. Not sure what I mean, myself, but," His voice trailed off before he gave a warm smile and patted Oliver on the forearm. "Don't mind me, lad. It's probably nothing more than the whims of an old mountain man."

Oliver felt a chill go down his spine as Daniel spoke. The man seemed genuinely scared, an emotion he rarely saw come from him. "Well, I'm glad he only got your arm either way. It should heal quickly, and I don't think you need stitches. I just want to watch it and ensure it doesn't get infected. That means take it easy with that arm. If you don't, then you'll have an irate doctor to deal with," Oliver warned with jest. He reached inside his medkit and pulled out bandages and a healing salve. The dressing was used to apply the ointment, and then, keeping the salved side down, he wrapped it around Daniel's arm until he covered all the minor puncture wounds. "There. You should be right as rain in a few days," Oliver said with a dimpled smile.

Daniel patted his shoulder and then pulled his sleeve back down. "Thank ya, Ollie. Glad to have all ya fancy east schooling helping my sorry ass."

Oliver chuckled as he put things away and stood up. "Someone's got to help your sorry ass, right? My professional opinion. Stop trying to fight wolves." He teased, then returned to where the coats hung to place his medicine bag below them.

"Oliver! Come get you a cup of coffee. Clyde broke out some jerky if you want some," Horace told him as he poured a cup and handed it to the doctor once he got near to him. "If'n ya don't mind, after you've drunk that and filled your belly, would you fetch us a couple buckets of snow to bring in for melting?"

"Thank you," Oliver said as he held the cup. The steam and the smell were rejuvenating in their own right, but taking that first sip was like heaven. "Sure, I don't mind at all," he agreed. He walked to one window and leaned against the wall to look out. The snow was still falling hard and in thick flakes. There was no visibility past the stable. The entire world outside was shades of gray. Typically, such wondrous winter scenes he found beautiful, but there was something about this place, about these woods, that made his skin crawl. Perhaps it was merely because of those eyes he'd thought he saw or how Daniel described the black wolf that attacked him. His bright blue orbs turned to look at the shed between the cabin and the stable where their kills' bodies lay. A sudden grip on his shoulder made him jump.

"You alright, Oliver? You seem a little jumpy?" Jake asked him with concern.

Oliver chuckled and rubbed his face. "No, I'm fine. You just startled me. What do you need?"

"I was wondering if you could fetch that snow now. We used up all we had in our canteens to make the coffee, and I'd like to wash up a bit before we hit the hay for the evening," Jake answered. His strong-featured face was dirty, and most had dried blood on their hands from field dressing.

"Yeah, sure. It'll just take me a moment," Oliver assured him before he put down the coffee cup and donned his coat again. A few buckets were next to the stove, so he grabbed those before heading out. An uneasy feeling settled deep in his spine, making him extra cautious once outside. His eyes looked everywhere around him, even behind him, to ensure he wasn't being watched or worse.

CHAPTER TWO

~ II ~

THE STRANGER

Oliver wrapped his scarf around his neck tighter to keep the cold from his face. The wind was whipping the snow so hard it stung when it hit his skin. He picked up the two buckets and walked away from the cabin to gather fresh snow, not trampled snow. Since they'd covered the front yard with human and horse prints, Oliver went around to the side of the house where he was sure there would be untouched snow. As soon as he'd turned the corner, that feeling of being watched intensified. It wasn't just the cold that gave him goosebumps as his skin tingled with fear. He paused momentarily, still in a world swirling with wind and white.

He couldn't see anything through the snow, trees, and dark, but that didn't stop the feeling from going away. Oliver knelt down and gathered snow into the buckets after not hearing any sound, not that he could hear well with the wind. He realized it would have been less work if he grabbed something to scoop the snow up.

"Excuse me," a voice came out of the dark behind him. Oliver fell into the snow as he turned to see who'd sneaked behind him. Standing, a man dressed in a long black coat and hat looked at him with concern. Behind him was a colossal beast of a horse whose color was indiscernible in the dark. "I'm terribly sorry. I didn't mean to frighten you," he said as he stepped forward and offered a hand.

"Holy shit. You terrified the hell out of me," Oliver answered him as he took the hand up. Before addressing this stranger, he dusted himself off and took deep breaths to calm his heart. Could this man have been following them for a while? If so, why? Oliver liked to think that he wouldn't be stupid enough to come up and say something if he was planning on robbing them. Then again, perhaps he knew that pretending to be a harmless stranger would be the best ploy to get what he wanted. He realized he was overthinking things and needed to respond. "Did you get caught in the storm as well?" Oliver asked curiously and hoped he didn't sound too suspicious.

"A little, yeah. I wasn't expecting that beautiful snow shower from earlier would get so angry," the man explained with a toothy smile. "The name's Jack Townsend. Just Jack will do," Jack introduced himself and held a gloved hand out in the introduction.

Oliver returned the handshake. "Jack, I'm Oliver Murdock." Oliver noticed the man's accent differed from the one he knew. "Where are you from, Jack? Have you been following us for a while now?" he couldn't help but ask.

"It's the accent, isn't it?" he asked. "I'm from England, originally. You could say I'm a bit of an adventurer now," Jack answered with whimsy. "I followed your trail more accurately, hoping to find friendly faces. Do you mind if I wait out the storm with you? I know it's a lot to ask from a stranger, but I'm afraid I'm rather at your mercy in this storm."

"Oh, um," Oliver began as he turned to look at the cabin as if he could see through it to the others. "You'd have to ask Jake. He's been the leader of our hunting party, but unless he feels a good reason to say no, I can't imagine he would. He will probably have questions. I hope you understand. I'll take you to him if you want to hitch your horse at the stable while I fill these buckets with snow."

"Brilliant. Thank you, Oliver. Come on, Wraith, let's get you hitched," Jack spoke to his massive stallion and led him toward the stable. He whistled a melancholy tune as he left Oliver to his task. Oliver quickly filled the two buckets with snow and headed back toward the front of the cabin. This Jack seemed nice enough, but Oliver couldn't shake a weary feeling. He stood at the door and waited for Jack to rejoin him before opening the door and entering the cabin. "Hey, Jake! We got a visitor," Oliver softly yelled to Jake, who got up from the card game he played with Horace.

"A visitor? Out here in this weather on this mountain?" Jake asked with natural suspicion as he peered around the doctor to look at this man. "What do you want?"

Jack moved to stand beside Oliver just inside the door. As he removed his hat, he had a beaming smile on his scruffy face. The man's hair wasn't long, but it wasn't short either. It was an ashy dark brown color with curls going wildly everywhere. "My name is Jack Townsend. I will assume I am in the same predicament as you, fine gentlemen. I became caught unawares in this blizzard, and I'm hoping for your charity to let me wait it out in the warmth of this cabin." Everyone was in tense silence before Jack continued, "If I may. I caught a couple of conies today, and I'm happy to share them with you all for dinner tonight."

"What's the hell is a cony?" Emmanuel asked in confusion.

"Rabbits. In England, we call them conies," Jack explained simply. Emmanuel seemed confused by that, but he was used to explaining some odd words he used to the Americans.

The dinner gift wasn't enough to persuade Jake to let the man stay. "What's your business in these parts, Jack?"

He asked gruffly as he sized the man up and down, though it was hard to determine with all the winter gear still on.

"As I told the delightful Oliver here, I'm what you'd call an adventurer. I've traveled the world, and now my feet have led me here. That's the truth, good sir," Jack said politely with a hopeful look.

Delightful? Oliver didn't need the compliment to be persuaded into vouching for Jack. "I think we should let him stay. It's worse out there. Sending him off could be sending him to his death, Jake. I don't think any of us want that on our conscience," Oliver was a pushover when it came to helping others. He was a little wary of this man, but that was only because he was wary before he asked for help. Had it not been for those terrifying eyes, Sid wouldn't have worried at all.

Jack turned toward his savior, put his palms flat together, and gave him a thankful bow. However, no matter what Oliver was like, Jack thought he was devilishly handsome, though that was neither here nor there. He had a relatively good nose for people's characters; this Oliver seemed like the pinnacle of what most would consider a 'good man.' Truthfully, the integrity that... that... well, illuminated from him was almost enough to burn his own blackened soul.

Jake rubbed his hand through his hair before sighing, "Yeah, alright, he can stay till the storm blows over. Just be aware that I'll toss your sorry ass back into the cold if you do anything suspicious."

Jack nodded fervently. "Yes, I quite understand. Thank you for your kindness, sir." His hackles raised a little at the threatening tone used against him, but he realized why the man thought it was necessary. He had to keep himself from revealing the slightly arrogant smile tugging at the corner of his lips. He knew he shouldn't think this way, but he was confident enough in his skills and abilities to understand that these men wouldn't stand a chance against him.

Oliver looked around the cabin and noticed one of their numbers was missing. "Where did Daniel go?" he asked with concern.

"Said he wasn't feeling so good. Probably the shock of defending himself from a wolf. We told him to take the bedroom and lie down for a bit. I'm sure he'll be alright in no time," Emmanuel answered him around a mouthful of jerky.

"Show some manners, kid. Eat with your mouth closed," Clyde scolded him while he shuffled cards.

"A wolf attacked him?" Jack asked with a hint of urgency. "Did it happen to be a black wolf?" They fell silent as they stared at the stranger, unsure whether to be worried about that statement. "I was being stalked by one. At least it felt that way a day ago. My horse sensed it before it could get too close. Eventually, I lost it. I'm sorry that it found you and attacked one of your friends," he explained.

"Yes, it was a black wolf. Daniel kept the kill to skin it and sell the fur," Oliver finally answered since it didn't seem like any others cared. A flutter of an unknown feeling briefly tickled his insides as he looked around and saw the looks on his friends' faces. The tenseness in the air grew thicker.

Jack merely nodded at that answer, though his mind was whirling with thoughts."Well, I will unpack my horse before I get out of this warm coat. And, as promised, I'll clean those conies, er, rabbits for us to cook on the fire." Jack said as he put his hat back on and walked back outside. He headed for the stable first to remove Wraith's tack and get him settled in the stable, away from the other horses as much as possible. The stallion could be a vicious creature if the mood struck him. "You behave, alright?" Jack ordered him as he rubbed the giant horse's muzzle and kissed him on the nose. That horse was honestly his best friend. They'd been through a lot together, and he couldn't imagine life without the surly beast.

Jack then took the conies and went outside to clean them as fast as possible. They were ready to put on a spit and cook over the fire for all to enjoy, but Jack first needed to check on something. He followed the footprints around the area to determine where the men had stashed their kills since they obviously weren't in the stable. It didn't take him long to figure they had likely put them in the shed. He opened the door to the metallic smell of blood and death. Any smell like those always made his more primal side wake up. The black wolf was easy to spot, so he approached the body and knelt above it. He took hold of the head and opened its mouth. On the roof of its mouth, there was an odd burned-looking mark. "You bastard. What in the devil's name have you done?" he asked, barely above a whisper.

Maybe it wasn't too late. Perhaps the man wasn't affected by the bite, but that was hoping for too much. "I told you, you'd get yourself killed one day. Not surprised I was right."Jack drew a wicked-looking dagger across his palm until blood appeared. Then, he held his hand over the wolf's mouth, and when the blood dripped into it, he murmured, "Quas eieci te vero mortis."

"What are you doing?" Oliver asked from the doorway where Jack had neglected to shut the door. The stranger turned around. An appalled and confused look covered his face. It looked like Jack's eyes were black, but as quickly as he thought that, he realized they were normal, albeit the grayest eyes he'd ever seen.

Well, this was awkward. Perhaps not as embarrassing as when a nun at a Catholic monastery in Spain caught him using a man's intestines to make a pentagram around his body, but it was still awkward. Now it was time to lie his way out of this. "I was curious if the wolf was the same one that tried attacking me. It is."

Oliver gave him a queer look, "That language you were speaking was Latin, was it not?" He knew what Latin sounded like since it was commonly used in medical terminology. Still, he didn't know how to speak it fluently. That fluttery feeling was growing stronger now, and it was a warning of danger.

Jack pointed slowly at the man and made a deduction, "You're a doctor or a scientist of some sort, aren't you?" He tried to look like he was more amused than annoyed at the doctor's knowledge. "Yes, it was Latin. I spent part of my childhood in a Catholic boys' school. I've retained some Latin they taught us there." He hoped that was enough explanation for Oliver to leave the conversation alone.

"Ah, I see. I'm a doctor, yes. Do you mind me asking what it was you said? I'm rather curious," Oliver asked as he looked hard and confidently at Jack. He couldn't translate it, but perhaps he could tell if Jack was lying about what it meant.

"No, no, not at all. I'm afraid it isn't fascinating, though, as all I said was," A yell cut off whatever lie about fell from Jack's lips. "What's going on?" Jack asked, more than happy about the distraction.

Oliver looked towards the cabin, "I don't know, but I'm going to go check." He said and then took off at a run back to the door. Thankfully, the shed wasn't far from the cabin, so it wasn't hard to find in the snowfall.

Jack followed him. There wasn't a sinking feeling in his stomach, but he had a feeling he knew what was going on inside, and it would not be pretty. Jack prepared himself for the shitshow that was about to happen. If his assumption were correct, it would be the same song and dance he experienced last time. A deep sigh escaped him as he caught up with Oliver, who was already inside the door.

Oliver paused at the entranceway, at the chaotic scene unfolding before him. With a manic look on his face, Daniel tried to stab Jake with his hunting knife. Jake was holding him off, but barely, even as Horace and Clyde tried to pull the old mountain man off him. Oliver had never seen such a crazed look in Daniel's eyes before. It was terrifying. It was as if a demon had taken him over and made him into some sort of crazed killer.

"Don't just stand there. We need to get the old man off of him," Jack said as he practically threw his coat and hat off so he could get into the fray himself. He squeezed his way into taking Horace's place to grab hold of the old man's arm.

Oliver shook himself out of it and jumped in to help. Instead of assisting Daniel, he tried to help Jake and get him away from their crazed friend. It took several minutes with all the men mixed in the fight getting thrown this way and that, but finally, they could get Daniel off of Jake. Clyde knocked the knife out of his hand while Jack could put him in a locked grip and dragged him back to the bedroom. Roughly, he threw the man in and shut the door. It swung outside to open, making it easy for Horace to grab a chair and block the entrance. Daniel was giving it his all to break through the barrier.

"What was that about?" Emmanuel asked with a frazzled look on his face.

After the taxing encounter, Horace, Clyde, Jake, and Oliver attempted to catch their breaths. Jack seemed alright and was busy putting more things in front of the door to keep Daniel in. "I don't know. Daniel came out of the room. He seemed to be in a daze. His skin was pale and sweating profusely. We were all asking if he was alright and needed something to drink, and without warning, he came charging at Jake. None of us even noticed the knife in his hand at first," Clyde answered as he moved to pick up a knocked-over chair and sat on it by the table.

Oliver examined Jake to see if Daniel hurt him, but it didn't appear the knife had made contact. "What would cause him to do such a thing? Does anyone have any idea?" Jake asked.

Jack kept quiet as he leaned against one wall with his

arms crossed. Without winter wear, they could better see him. He stood a little shorter than Oliver. From how his clothes strained in certain places, it was a good guess he was physically fit. His scruffy face was attractively symmetrical. His eyes turned downward in thought as he tried to avoid eye contact with any of them. "The man acted like a rabid animal. Bit me like one too. Could it be rabies, Oliver?" Jake asked as he branded his left hand, with prominent teeth marks along the blade. A few points of blood had been spilled around it.

Jack's eyes shot up, looking over at Jake's hand. The action did not go unnoticed by Oliver, but he answered the hunter first. "Medically, no. Rabies does not start presenting itself for days to even a year sometimes. Then, it usually tingles around the wound, along with fever, headache, and nausea. If this is rabies, it is the most bizarre case I have ever seen in my life," was his answer. His bright blue eyes looked at Jack again to see the man looking more thoughtful than before.

"Until Daniel calms down, there isn't much we can do right now. I suggest we give him time to cool off, then I can hopefully examine him better and see what is afflicting him. I suggest we all try to relax in the meantime." Oliver looked at everyone in the room and then moved over to where Jack was standing. The others quickly went back to what they were doing before.

CHAPTER THREE

~ III ~

THE STORM RAGES INSIDE

Jack looked up at Oliver as he neared and stood up straighter while uncrossing his arms. "What can I do for you, Sir Oliver?" he asked in a cheeky voice, with a carefree smile.

Oliver stood close to him so the others wouldn't overhear what they were saying. "Cut the shit, Jack. You know more about what's happening than you're letting on," he accused in an angry whisper. He'd vouched for this man, but now he wondered if that had been a good idea. Jack argued with him, but Oliver cut him off. "Stop, just stop. Be straight with me."

"With you looking like that? Sorry, darling, I don't think I can do that," Jack said flirtatiously, with a wink for the doctor.

That effectively threw Oliver for a loop. Did this man

just flirt with him? That was bold of him, considering Jack didn't know him from Adam. He could be one of those men that took great offense at being flirted with by another man and would even go to blows over it. Oliver wasn't offended but had conflicting feelings about it. He'd never admitted it to anyone and barely acknowledged it, but Oliver was attracted only to men. If his mother or, God forbid, his father had ever suspected, they'd have kicked him out immediately. It was a part of him that he simply did not acknowledge, so for Jack to be so open about his homosexuality was astonishing.

"Cat got your tongue? I might have to be jealous of that proverbial cat," Jack continued without mercy. He was aware of the stigma and the reactions most people gave when finding out a man was gay. Well, gay wasn't entirely correct. Jack preferred to label himself as greedy.

"What? No. Stop trying to throw me off guard," Oliver growled at him with some irritation, though his cheeks were blushing now. "Now tell me what in the hell is going on. What's wrong with Daniel?"

The charming smile dropped from Jack's face, "What in the hell is right." He ran a hand through his curly locks and gave a sigh. "Look, you wouldn't believe me if I told you. Instead of wasting my breath and our time, how about you just help me with anything I might ask of you," he suggested. Oliver almost laughed out loud, but Jack gave him a severe look. "I mean it, Oliver. I don't know if

I can figure out how to cure this. Honestly, I'm not sure where to even start."

Oliver gave him a cock-eyed look. "How about you try me? See if I believe you. I'm not stupid, Jack. I have a good feeling this has something to do with that damned wolf."

Jack stood up straighter and almost intimidating as he stared hard into Oliver's eyes. "No. I don't care if you don't trust me, but this is not something I will elaborate on. If I were you, I would drop the matter immediately." It wasn't a threat, but it wasn't *not* a threat either. "Believe me. I am keeping you and the other's best interests in mind." His voice was firm, but he could see that Oliver wanted to argue with him. Jack set his jaw a little tighter and stared with more intimidation at him to stop him from speaking. Jack wasn't the sort that liked to repeat himself many times. Had he not already found the doctor pleasant and attractive, he would have been tempted to take care of this problem the easiest way possible.

Oliver wanted to argue that he could take the truth no matter what, but something about Jack's eyes kept him from doing it. Yes, he heard the harsh tone of the man's voice, but those eyes kept his lips shut. The longer Oliver looked into Jack's eyes, the more dread overcame him. They were dark and foreboding, warning this man was dangerous and that something terrible would befall him if he continued to press for more information. Oliver thought about how he had assumed Jack's eyes had turned black in the shed. He almost expected them to turn completely black, but they didn't. "Fine, keep your secrets. What can I do to help Daniel?" he asked instead.

Jack looked about the room in silence for a moment. "First, I want you to monitor Jake. Ensure he doesn't start acting weird or complaining about not feeling good."

"Okay, why?" Oliver asked suspiciously. "Is it because Daniel bit him and broke the skin?" Jack's brows knitted together before he shook his head.

"You need to stop guessing right on things seriously. Trust me. This is one situation where you'll be much happier not to guess everything right." He meant it earnestly, but his voice was light with humor. "For now, just relax and act as normal as you can. I'm going to," he cut himself off mid-sentence.

"What? What are you," Oliver urged him to continue, but Jack cut him off by holding a finger up his lips.

"Do you hear that?" the stranger asked curiously.

Oliver knocked his finger away from his lip as if swatting at a fly. "Hear what? I hear nothing."

"That's what I was afraid of. C'mon." Jack turned on his heels and headed toward the bedroom where they were holding Daniel. A steady stream of pounding had been coming from that room recently, and now it was silent. Jack removed all the barriers he had put in front of the door to keep Daniel from getting out and trying to kill one of them again. "Help me," he asked Oliver when the man came up beside him with a bewildered look.

Oliver said nothing as he helped the odd stranger move the small table before the door. Then, he slowly removed the chair under the doorknob and opened the door. On the floor, in spread-eagle fashion, was Daniel. He looked even worse than before, and Oliver couldn't tell if he was breathing. "Daniel, hey, Daniel. Can you hear me?" he asked as he knelt beside the unconscious man. His hand searched for a pulse as he leaned down with his cheek over the man's mouth and nose to see if he could feel any breathing. "He's still alive, but his pulse is weak, and his breathing sounds labored," Oliver diagnosed as the others looked in the room.

"Let's get him onto the bed," Jack suggested as he grabbed under the man's arms and hauled him up to his feet with little trouble.

Impressed by the man's strength, Oliver grabbed Daniel's legs so they could lift him onto the bed and arrange him in a more comfortable position. "What is wrong with him? Is it rabies? Is it something else more contagious? Should we worry about getting this?" Emmanuel asked quickly and nervously as he backed away from the room like he was afraid that being that close would be enough to get him just as sick.

"Calm yourself, young man. We know nothing about it yet. Let's just try to stay calm. Panicking over it will not help anyway," Horace tried to assure the young man, though his soothing words didn't help.

While Jack tried reassuring the other men at ease, Oliver sat next to Daniel. He looked him over for any signs or clues that would give him a better idea of what illness they were dealing with. Daniel was running a fever with a slow and erratic heartbeat. He was sweating profusely now, and there seemed to be some rash on his neck. Oliver hadn't noticed that before and turned him to expose his back and neck.

"What the hell?" he whispered as he saw a large, pustular knot. It was a sickly phlegm yellow color, comparable to a giant pimple, and the size of a half-dollar coin. He knelt down closer to look at it better. Around the head was a ring of black, the signs of necrosis, but Oliver had never seen that happen so quickly. An angry red spread out from around it after that. "Dear God in heaven, what is," he began to ask, but the thin layer of skin broke and covered the doctor in sour juices. Oliver jumped back with a yelp and smacked at his face to get the disgusting fluid off him. Some of it had landed in his mouth. That sent him to the corner, where he conveniently found a pot to retch in.

Jack turned in time to see what disgusting thing had happened. Quickly, he turned Daniel onto his back to press his neck against the bed before moving over to Oliver. He put a hand on his shoulder and patted his back comfortingly. "Easy there, my darling. You alright?" he asked with concern.

"No, absolutely not. I don't know what the hell that was, but it got in my mouth," Oliver answered angrily as he wiped his mouth.

Jack's entire body tensed and stilled at the same time. He practically pulled the doctor around to face him. "It got in your mouth? You're sure?" A confused and concerned look crossed his face at how Jack handled him.

"Yeah. Why do you think I'm over here throwing up? I'm a doctor, for God's sake. I've seen worse than that, maybe not weirder, but more disgusting."

"Dammit, Okay. It's okay. You'll be fine," Jack stated in a way that wasn't a hundred percent confident. He remembered when it was hard even to pretend to care about people. Jack found it easier to care for others now, even if it was mainly pretending. However, he was starting to feel he needed to protect this doctor he barely knew for some damn reason.

Oliver gave the scruffy man a disbelieving look. "Why do I not feel confident with how you said that? Will you now tell me what's going on? Are our lives in danger? Please, give me something. I'm a doctor. I might help more than you're giving me credit for."

Jack took a deep breath as he shifted from foot to foot. "I'm not sure there is anything you could do medically that could help. Perhaps treating the symptoms will help slow things down, but I've never tried that before." This was not the first time he'd seen something like this. He hadn't tried to stop the first time he'd seen it. This would be a first for him, but if he succeeded, this disease would never reenter the world. The disease didn't spread in the first place because everyone in the small village who contracted it died before it could spread to other people. "I'll be honest with you, Oliver. If I can't stop it, the most important thing will be to ensure it doesn't leave this cabin. Otherwise," he said. Somberly he looked at the doctor with a bleak but apologetic look.

Oliver fell very silent and stationary as he processed the information that Jack had just given him. It didn't matter that he thought this man knew more than he was letting on. Lives were at stake, including his own. "Alright. To let you know, I have a lot of questions, but we need to act fast. What else besides the symptoms Daniel has shown?" he asked calmly.

"Come with me," Jack said as he took hold of Oliver's forearm and led him out of the room and away from prying ears. The small closet was the only other private place.

"Monitor him, lads. I need to borrow the good doctor for just a few moments," Jack told the others in the room and then closed the door behind himself and Oliver. "For your own benefit, I will not answer questions. I will only tell you what I think you need to know to help slow this thing down. Got it?" he asked, but it was more of a command.

Oliver gave a long sigh. He wanted to know what they were working against, as much as Jack knew, but he knew it was a losing battle when he saw one. "Alright, fine, fine, but if I live through this, I want some proper answers from you," he countered with his own terms.

Jack gave the doctor a tight-lipped grin and a slap on the arm. "Trust me, buddy. If you live through this, you'll have many more questions," the stranger said cryptically. "Now," he slapped his hands together and rubbed them fast enough to create heat from the friction, "first things first, the symptoms you might treat. The first one seems innocent enough. It begins with a headache. One that keeps getting worse and worse. You might ease it with some pain medicine if you have any. The second is extreme lethargy. Which is undoubtedly what sent your mountain man friend to bed. After that, this is a crucial part. When a person wakes up, they become very violent, almost rabid. I never saw a person go crazy that didn't first go to sleep when they started feeling bad, so if we can keep people awake, that could help us. After the rabid-like symptoms start, a fever normally follows. Finally, those boils that popped are the last symptom before death inevitably comes." he spoke slowly, so Oliver would clearly understand his fate.

Oliver was quick-witted and got the news loud and clear. His heart sank for a moment. Daniel was a good man, and he'd always been friendly to him. In fact, if he'd known the old mountain man longer, he might have even seen him as the father figure he never had. He would have to mourn for Daniel later. "So, something for headaches, lethargy, and fever. I don't have much in my medicine bag, but I have something for all those. I guess I should get myself out two doses of each since it seems like Jake, and then I will be the next victim." His voice wasn't pessimistic, just realistic.

Jack put both hands on his shoulder and gave him a shake. "I will do everything within my power to ensure you all get out of this alive. I promise." He gave the warmest and most assuring smile he could muster to Oliver. Jack didn't make promises often, but when he did, he kept them. "Let's get back to the others before," Before he could finish speaking, more screaming came from the bedroom. Jack got to the bedroom door before Oliver and raised his hand to keep him back until he opened the door first.

Oliver didn't have to be in front of Jack to see the hellish scene inside the room. Daniel had risen out of bed. It was him that the loudest screaming came from, though a few of the others were yelling in fear and panic. "Jack, what's happening to him?" he asked with concern trying to get past the man.

However, Jack proved a force he couldn't move. "There's nothing you can do for him now. Don't watch," Jack said as he easily could keep Oliver from getting by him by merely standing his ground. The blood-curdling screams from Daniel were nothing like any of them had ever heard. Anguish, pure, and unadulterated anguish was what he was wailing. The sound cracked and crumbled as it was also rising in octaves. The straining to make the sound made all his face and neck veins bulge and ripple. He scrambled in the meantime to rip his clothes off of him. It was almost a relief to have those screams muffled as he got his shirt pulled over his head.

The grotesque number of abscesses now covered his back like what was on his neck. They writhed, bulged, and seeped with sickly yellow pus. Daniel was stumbling around in pain and panic, with the shirt still over his head. The men in the room tried to escape him, but it wasn't a large room. Jack urged them to get to the door, but most were too worried about being close to Daniel to listen to him. Jake heard him and dove out of the room and behind Oliver as fast as possible. He was none too late, either, as the pustules ruptured with a loud bursting sound one by one. Clyde and Emmanuel were unlucky enough to be in the path of the bursting boils, but Horace got out of the room before he had any pop on him.

The rest of the boils on his body burst open in absolute horror. It wasn't just that the boils erupted like tiny dynamite sticks under them, but when they did so, they revealed how deep-rooted they were in his body. It was hard to decide which was more hideous. How these pustules exploded with a shower of yellow slimy liquid didn't seem possible. Or how the holes left were almost impeccably shaped like an empty honeycomb, with some spots overlapping. They bled a lot with blood that was dark and as vicious as molasses. Daniel's voice, damaged from the screaming he'd done, gave a final pathetic cry and fell face forward onto the floor. It was, without a doubt, the worst thing Oliver had ever seen in his life, and, doctor or not, the minced meat that remained almost made him vomit all over again.

"C'mon, you two, quick. Get out of here," Jack ordered Clyde and Emmanuel. They didn't waste any time leaving that room where pus puddles covered the floors. "Go quickly clean yourselves up and let Oliver know where pus hit you. I'm going to wrap the body in a bedsheet," he ordered them. They did not hesitate to listen. "I should help you with that," Horace offered, but Jack stopped him. "No, I should be the only one to handle this. Go clean up with the others, both of you, just in case. We can't be too sure," Jack stated firmly. Jake looked about to protest, so he added, "Don't worry about me. I'll be careful." Then he shooed them away, stepped inside the room, and shut the door.

"Well, you heard him. Let's make sure you all are fine, and let him take care of Daniel," Oliver said behind them. He was trying to erase that scene from his mind lest he focuses too hard on the fact that he might die that horrible death. "Clyde, Emmanuel, did any of that get in your mouths, eyes, an open wound?" Oliver asked. Then, he moved over to the men who had stripped out of their clothes and washed vigorously with the cold water he'd brought in.

The two men looked at each other briefly before Clyde answered, "Yes, I mean, I doubt it'll do anything, but I think some disgusting shit got in my eye. I rubbed it out quickly, though."

"Alright, just wash your face really well. Emmanuel, how about you?" Oliver turned to the younger man.

"Um, no. I'm good. Just got on my clothes. That was enough," Emmanuel answered quickly.

Perhaps too quickly for Oliver's liking, but it wasn't like he would accuse him of lying. They had enough problems without throwing accusations at each other. "As the doctor here, I have a few instructions I need you guys to follow without fail, okay? If you get a headache, tell me. If you feel really sleepy, tell me. Until we know more about what is going on, none of us must go to sleep. Watch each other. Horace, maybe you could make us another pot of coffee to help, eh?"

"What's going on here, Oliver? Who is that man, and why does it seem like he's the only one with knowledge of what just happened to poor Daniel? The way he's acting like it's just us that has to worry about following Daniel to the grave is foreboding, and I don't care for it," Jake demanded.

Oliver held his hands up in defense. "I really don't know more than you guys do about Jack. However, I can tell you he's the only one that has maybe dealt with what we're dealing with now. So, foreboding or not, he's the best chance we have to make it through this." None of them seemed convinced by his words, so he sighed deeply and tried a different tactic. "Don't forget that there are also more of us than him. If Jack does anything that would harm us, we can easily subdue him. Right?"

The men felt a little better at that thought. Everyone thought they were strong, so they preferred to believe they could take care of one man. Even if that man was rather intimidating. Jake, Clyde, Horace, and Emmanuel looked at each other to confirm they were on the same level before Jake turned to Oliver. "I suppose you are right. We're not exactly in a situation where we can be picky about our help. If," he had to stop to swallow the bile in his throat before he spoke more, "If what happened to poor Daniel is fated for us, then, may God have pity on our souls."

The rest of the men nodded at that brief prayer as they said their own silent ones. The creak of the bedroom door opened and caught their attention as the man in question came out. He didn't look frazzled. "I have taken care of the body. How are you all holding up? Oliver, did any of them get anything in their mouths, wounds, or anything else?" Jack asked curiously as he moved to the bucket of water and washed his hands in it. "I will take this bucket of water out and fill it with new snow to melt. We don't want to drink any of this accidentally," he said helpfully.

The tension in the room was apparent, but that didn't bother him. These men were scared, and rightly so. He picked up the bucket and headed outside without bothering with his coat. He tossed the water out; it still steamed as it hit the cold winter air. If there was one blessing, the storm had slowed down a bit. He hoped he could stop this plague before the storm stopped entirely. Otherwise, Jack didn't know these people or care to know them all. Still, right now, they were his responsibility. It was up to him to ensure that none escaped here to continue spreading the plague. Jack moved to a fresh patch of snow, gathered more into the bucket, and returned inside. He set the bucket down near the fire so it would melt quickly.

Oliver approached Jack and spoke closely to him, "Clyde thinks that some of that pus got into his eyes. Emmanuel says that he doesn't think that anything got into his system, but,"

"But what, Oliver?" Jack encouraged him.

"I don't know. I'm too paranoid, but it felt as if Manny was lying about that," he answered, rubbing the back of his neck. A thought began. "I can't say that I know him all that well. Not as well as I know the others or as I did Daniel, but I don't want to assume the lad would lie outright."

Jack gave the boy a piercing look. "We'll just have to be sure to keep a close eye on him. On everyone but especially him." His smoky gray eyes watched Horace as he got some coffee back over the fire.

"Do you know the incubation period of this illness? Daniel was bit by that wolf but didn't fall ill until we got here. Which is still quite fast for any virus. Granted, I've never heard or seen something like this. It feels biblical in nature." Oliver said. His stomach churned violently, thinking of his exposure.

Jack looked at the handsome man and sighed before answering, "I don't have a firm answer for that, but yes, it is fast and varies for everyone." He responded honestly before he moved to walk behind the doctor and gave his shoulders a gentle squeeze. "How are you feeling, though? Any headache yet?"

The squeeze of his shoulders actually felt pretty good. His back and shoulders were so tense that they'd gone numb to the pain a while ago. A sigh of pleasure escaped him at the strong fingers pressing against the points that hurt the most. "That felt good, thank you. I don't have a headache yet, nor do I feel any overt lethargy," Oliver answered.

Jack pulled up a chair next to them and pressed Oliver into it. "That's good, at least." He happily continued to give the man's shoulders a nice rub. He'd never been good with soothing words, so he learned that touch was much easier when he wanted to convey comfort.

The slight squeeze to the shoulder was one thing, but now he was getting an entire shoulder rub. It made him self-conscious, but it also felt really good. He noticed then the odd look that Clyde was giving him and Jack, so he straightened up and moved his shoulders away."What now? Surely there's something we can do besides sit around and wait." Oliver asked with some impatience. He wanted this whole thing to end.

"I am trying to figure that out as we go, actually. I witnessed this plague before, but I had as much knowledge on how to stop it then as I do now. I have a book I am going to look through that might help," Jack answered. He shouldn't relish playing guinea pig with the men once they get sick. However, his darker side found the prospect of experimenting with human bodies again alluring. "For now, you keep the others calm, and I'm going to do some heavy reading," Jack was not kidding as he moved over to his bag and pulled out an old weathered book that was a good two to three inches thick and sat down.

CHAPTER FOUR

~ IV ~

A MATTER OF TIME

Fear spread over the following hours. With the tensions high, the men started bickering and clashing over the smallest things. Oliver was doing what he could to put out fires, but mentally he was worn down. Emmanuel seemed to be the most on edge. Just looking at him could cause him to lash out. Oliver, being cautious already, watched him closer. It was easy to think he was just irritated because of the situation, but anger was one of the symptoms to look out for. That went against what Jack had said about people not turning violent until after they had gone to sleep and woke back up, but that didn't mean he couldn't be wrong about it.

During that time, Jack held up his ancient-looking book, reading it in a corner. There were a few things and items that he read about that might work. Still, it would be more challenging than herding cats to convince these people that cures were the only way to save their lives.

He sighed and let his head fall back against the wall with a thud. It would be much easier to end all this now in the safest way he knew to keep the disease from spreading. However, to do that would mean that he didn't try all he could to cure them. He was sure that taking the straightforward way out would only add another black mark to his soul, which was the opposite of what he had been trying to achieve for years. A sound of pain caught his attention, and he looked up in time to see Jake give his head a rub.

Jack wasn't the only person to notice it. Oliver heard it and walked over to the man. "You have a headache, Jake?" he asked as he felt the leader's forehead. "You're a little clammy and warm. I'm going to give you some medicine now."

"Don't fuss over me, boy. I'm feeling alright," Jake stated. It was not shocking that he was trying to act strong.

He would not fool Oliver, though. Oliver got the medicine he'd sat out and began to dosage out what he wanted Jake to have. "You can lie to yourself all you want, Jake, but you're taking this medicine. Or would you rather see yourself reach the same untimely end that Daniel did?" His voice was firm and commanding. Jake grunted and growled at him, no doubt irritated to listen to a young man, but he took what he was told to take.

With the medicine delivered and Jake strongly advised

to drink more coffee to stay awake, Oliver moved over to check on Jack. He tried to get a peek at the book he was reading, but odd drawings and a language he couldn't make out were all that could be seen. "How are you coming along?" he asked.

Jack closed his eyes momentarily and heard someone approach when he was spoken to. The book was shut quickly and as nonchalantly as possible. He didn't need a good doctor to be able to figure out what he was reading. "My eyes hurt, but I might have something. However, there are some things I need to do before I try this approach." He didn't go into details, and he didn't plan to.

"I can imagine your eyes hurt. What are you reading anyway? I don't believe I've ever seen a medical book like that? Is it something special from England?" Oliver asked curiously as he tried to look at the book's cover for a title.

Jack put the book under his arm as he stood up. "Yeah, something like that anyway. How are the others doing? Do you think you and them will be alright while I go out to find what I'm looking for?" he asked. Then, he twisted his back to get the knots out. A few good cracks along his spine made him sigh in pleasure. Shit, he was old, but he couldn't imagine that age was catching up to him yet.

"Um, we'll be alright, but do you need any help gathering supplies? It might not be as bad out there, but it could still be pretty easy for someone to get lost out in that snow," Oliver pointed out and was ready to go with him to help get whatever he required. He was merely curious about what Jack needed to get from the woods. If Jack went by himself, he might take a sneak peek at the book he'd been reading. Something about the swirling-looking words made him want to read it better.

"No, I'd rather you stay here with them. Make sure things don't get out of control. They shouldn't as long as no one falls asleep, but I would feel better to know that you're here to watch out," Jack answered as he put the book back into his bag before he donned his coat. The bag was draped over his shoulder before he put his hat back on. "I will not have to go far, I don't think. If you happen to need me, call me. I should be able to hear you," he explained, then headed out the door into the night. The first place he made a stop was the shed. He needed to gather some of the blood from the creature and put it in a small jar. Then, he needed a couple of plants, which would be harder to find, thanks to so much snow on the ground. Jack headed out into the dark woods and disappeared into the shadows.

Oliver watched out the window as Jack headed into the woods and disappeared there. He was a bit irritated Jack had taken the book with him, though if some of those doodles he'd barely seen were pictures of plants, Oliver could understand why he took it with him. The doctor might ask to read the book when the man returns. He doubted he could, but it wouldn't hurt to ask, right? His focus now needed to stay on the other men and himself. He was feeling a bit of a headache forming behind his eyes. Oliver would not take any chances and got himself out a dose of the aspirin he'd given the others for headaches. More time had passed than he thought since he'd started staring out the window. "How is everyone doing? Does anyone need anything? Wait... where is Jake? He was sitting there a moment ago," Oliver asked with concern as he stretched his sore muscles and turned away from the window.

Clyde and Emmanuel looked around and then at each other before they shrugged and looked back at the doctor with uncertain looks. "I'm not sure. He was there." Clyde answered him.

Emmanuel's face lit up in remembrance for a moment. "I heard him tell Horace that he was going to step outside for a moment to take a leak. I haven't seen him step back in, though."

Horace stood up and stretched. "Aye, that he did. He should have been back in by now, though. I'll go look for him." He offered as he moved to the back door and opened it. "Jake! Where are you at, Jake!?" He waited a moment for an answer before calling out again. "Jake! Answer me! We're all getting worried about you," the kind old man added. There was a sound from around the corner of the house. Horace turned and looked back at the others before he stepped out to see if it was Jake. Oliver joined him as a bad feeling sank into his stomach. Horace stepped around the corner and immediately saw Jake lying face down in the snow beside the house. "Jake! Oliver, over here!" he said as he ran through the snow to get to the man's side.

Oliver ran the rest of the way out of the door and to the side of the house. Guilt weighed on his shoulders as he realized he hadn't kept as close an eye on Jake as he should have. His suspicion of Emmanuel had held most of his attention. He had forgotten that Jake was the one that had likely been infected next to Daniel. "I'm sorry. I should have been paying more attention. He was injured by Daniel, so be careful around him, Horace." Oliver warned Horace as he caught up to him.

"I believe Daniel bit him hard enough to draw blood. I also believe Daniel spit at him as he was trying to rip his face off," Horace contributed. A look of disgust was given to the memories of that fight. He was usually peaceful and didn't understand why so many men quickly went into fists with each other. However, seeing two people he considered friends go to blows was worse. Daniel hadn't only been fighting but had actively tried to kill Jake. "Not a lot we can do now. Should we wake him up?" Horace asked.

Oliver tiptoed closer to Jake and tried pulling down his shirt's collar to see if he could find any boils on his skin. A sound of disappointment was pressed fast through his nose as he moved back and stood up. "It looks like he has the start of them," he mumbled. "If only Jake wasn't so damn stubborn. He should have said he was that exhausted before going outside alone. We'll have to put him in the room with Daniel's body. Try not to wake him as we do. If he wakes up and turns violent, he could easily hurt one of us in his crazed mind," Oliver said as he moved to roll Jake over gently. Carefully, the two picked him up, brought him back inside, and carried him into the bedroom. It was depressing to leave him in here, but it wasn't as if there was anywhere else they could put him. Thank God Jack had cleaned up a little here, wrapped Daniel's body up, and laid it aside. They put Jake on the bed and then softly walked out. "Let's try to remember to be quiet. We don't want to wake him up accidentally," he suggested as he blocked the door again. Daniel hadn't been a small man, but Jake was obviously more muscular than the old man had been.

"How long till that strange man gets back?" Horace asked Oliver with concern.

Oliver shook his head as he gave Horace a pat on the shoulder. "I don't know. Let's pray it isn't too long."

In the cold and the snow, Jack was almost done and ready to head back to the cabin. A vial of blood, a couple of different herbs, and a few other little things in the bag with the book. Everything else he already had, like an elder raven's bones and a newborn calf's fur. "I hope nothing too exciting has happened since I left," Jack thought as he headed back toward the cabin. He'd never tried a healing spell on others before, but surely it would work.

Unfortunately, the excitement was getting started back at the cabin. Oliver and Horace had just settled back in front of the fire when there was a loud bang. "Dammit," Oliver swore as he got back up and ran to the bedroom door. The wooden boards were bouncing from the weight of each blow. "Jake, stop it!" Oliver yelled at him. The next hit was harder. So hard, in fact, that it managed to break loose one of those boards. Oliver was caught off guard as Jake focused on that board and was able to pry it out of the way. Horace ran up with a broom, and together they set it so it was stuck between the door and the opposite wall. "Good idea, Horace. Let's hope that holds."

Jake was still pounding on the door loudly, and it appeared he was putting his entire body into throwing himself against the door. The broom handle was holding up, but the chair was dislodged after a few hard hits. The crazed man was looking through the opening he'd made and tried to squeeze himself through it when he realized the door would not open. He was forcing himself so hard the wood dug into the flesh of his arm, shoulder, and the part of his head that barely fit.

"Jake, calm down. You're hurting yourself. Please, just stop, now!" Oliver urged the man. He would kill himself merely by trying to get through the door to attack them.

"Do you have anything that might calm him down?" Horace asked curiously.

"Nothing that would calm him down immediately without having to stick him with something. I don't know how we could hold him down long enough for me to do that safely," Oliver explained with hopelessness. Leaving him would be the safest thing, but the door cracked and creaked with abuse. "For now, let's find more things to keep the door firmly held shut," he suggested as he searched for other solid objects they could use.

Horace put the chair back under the handle. Suddenly there was a loud breaking sound, and wood fell around Horace. Oliver turned around to see what was happening and rushed to get to Horace's side, but he was too late. Jake was half sticking out of the larger hole in the door now and had Horace grasped around the neck with one arm. A glint of firelight sparked off a blade in his other hand before it was buried in the older man's chest. His eyes widened in shock and pain as his attempts to escape became feeble and slow. Horace's lifeless body fell to the floor with a thud. Jake could get through the door now and looked at Oliver with murderous intent. Oliver backed up and away from the man. Unlike Jake, who still had his knife, he was unarmed.

Jake awkwardly stumbled through the opening and lunged. His shirt caught on a largely broken splinter which pulled him back. He jerked and flailed in a fitful attempt to free himself. A guttural sound bubbled up from Jake's throat before a bloodline trickled out his mouth. He slumped to the floor on top of Horace's body. Jack was standing above him with a bloody dagger in his hand. Jake wasn't dead, though, and began to pull himself across the floor toward Oliver and Clyde. Blood flowing down his chin didn't seem to bother him. It also didn't bother Jack to step above him, grab a fistful of hair, and slice Jake's throat without hesitation.

"What the hell did you just do?!" Clyde demanded as he pulled his revolver on Jack.

Jack rolled his eyes as he sheathed his bloody dagger. "I did what had to be done. Which is something I doubt you could have despite it being the right choice." He answered as he walked up to Clyde until the gun was an inch away from his heart.

"You don't know that! Weren't you gonna go look for a cure or whatever?!" Clyde said as he cocked the trigger and held the gun at face level with Jack.

Oliver was now aware enough to intervene, and so he moved to get between them, "Hey! Stop it, you two. There's been enough death today." The questions Clyde was asking were ones he'd like to know himself. The way the man had so coldly cut their friend's throat was disturbing, but that didn't mean he wanted Clyde to shoot him.

Jack sighed deeply and rolled his eyes so hard his head moved back. Then, without flinching, he grabbed Clyde's gun and took it from his hands. "I do know that. Once you get to uncontrollable rage, there's no going back." He uncocked the pistol and shoved it against Clyde's chest to hand it back. "Now, one of you two help me get the bodies into the room with the other," Jack said in a commanding tone. He doubted it would harm them to leave the bodies where they were. Still, if he was wrong about the disease only being transmitted through body fluid, it was safer to keep them away. Clyde seemed shocked that he was so deftly unarmed and stared at the stranger like he'd grown a second head.

"I'll help you with the bodies, Jack. Clyde, sit down and drink some coffee," Oliver spoke shakily. Jack removed his coat and moved over to the two bodies so he could join him. All he could think of was how he would tell their families. Daniel had been a loner, but everyone knew him. Jake had two little boys and a wife. Horace's wife had died years ago, but he had a daughter that was engaged to be married in the summer.

Jack could see the pain in the doctor's eyes. It was a pain he didn't understand, one he'd never felt and might never feel, but he could see how it affected others. "Hey," he got the doctor to look up at him with those striking blue eyes, "don't think about it right now. We're not out of the woods yet. There are still three of you that can be saved. Focus on that right now." Jack picked up Jake's legs, waited until Oliver picked up the other end, and dragged it to the bedroom.

"Why do you keep excluding yourself when talking?" Oliver had to ask. The way he acted as if he wasn't also in this situation was, at the very least, odd, and at the most, it unnerved him.

The man looked at Oliver as they carried Horace's body into the room. "Do I? I didn't notice. I'm a loner, so, It's rare that I'm in a group long enough to feel a part of it," Jack explained. He was a loner, that was for sure, but he didn't want to talk about him.

Oliver had to ask, "What will we do with their bodies when we're done here?" That assumed that they could do something.

"When you and the others are safe, we will worry about burning the bodies to make sure this doesn't spread," Jack explained as they put the body down next to the others and then walked out. "Okay, now that all the distractions are out of the way," he said annoyedly.

"Those were living people you're talking about so dismissively. Maybe try to show a little respect," Oliver said with anger as he grabbed the man's shoulder and turned him around to face him.

Those eyes were piercing in their judgment. Jack could stare down the barrel of a gun without batting an eyelash, but those eyes casting judgment on him he couldn't meet with his own. It'd been a long time since he'd been judged, and it had affected him. He didn't like it, not at all. "Right, respect," Jack gave a hollow apology. He quickly swept around Oliver to go to the table so he could begin getting things ready. Clyde was sitting there with his head in his hands, and Emmanuel, "Hang on a moment," Jack said as he looked about, "Where is the young boy?"

Clyde lifted his head up and looked around. "I don't know," he answered without feeling.

"Shit," Jack said as he ran out the front door and looked for the kid. He didn't see him, so he ran to the stables, and sure enough, one horse was gone. Jack didn't waste time leading Wraith outside and mounting up without the saddle.

Oliver ran up to him just as he got on. "He made a run for it?"

"Yes, get on," Jack stated as he easily grabbed the doctor's arm and pulled him onto his steed. "Hang tight," he warned before spurring the draft toward the fresher trail. Thanks to all the fallen snow, it wasn't hard to know which direction the kid went.

Oliver had no choice but to go as he was pulled onto the enormous horse. His arms wrapped around Jack's waist and held onto him for dear life, almost. He wasn't bad at horseback riding, but going at this pace with no saddle was not in his skill set. For now, he focused on keeping his balance so he wouldn't make either fall off. The snow glittered in the moonlight as it was kicked up by hooves flying over it.

Wraith was a reliable horse and the only horse that Jack would ever trust. He was not at all concerned about Wraith stumbling or falling down. That left him to follow the trail until it ended when the horse the kid took was found lying on its side and whining with pain. The broken leg was visible, as were the footprints running away from the fallen creature. "He can't be far," Jack said, continuing after Emmanuel. If he was infected, he'd likely die trying to get back down from this mountain in the winter, but Jack would rather be sure and not leave anything up to fate.

It wasn't long before they saw the boy weaving in and out of the trees, heading down the hill. Jack moved Wraith to catch up beside him and cut him off in front. Emmanuel skidded to a stop and tried to run a different way. Jack slid off his mount and quickly tackled the kid, "Oh no, you're not going anywhere."

Oliver was less graceful getting off the giant beast but managed and ran to help. "What the hell do you think you're doing, Manny? Why did you run?" he asked as he helped to keep the kid from running. While fighting to get free, his clothes moved enough that Oliver could see a couple of boils on his lower back. "You're infected; you knew you were infected," he stated as a fact and not an accusation.

Jack was not as patient as Oliver in trying to get this kid to stop trying to escape. "Stop moving now, kid, or I won't hesitate to kill you. For all we know, you're in a rage right now," he threatened and pulled his still-bloody blade so he could see he meant it.

That got the kid to stop. He'd run after he watched Jake get his throat slashed by the man. The man had scared him before that, so he didn't doubt that he'd kill him as well without a second thought. "I'm sorry. I'm sorry. I got some of that disgusting stuff on my face and in my eyes as we dodged Daniel. I didn't want to die. I just don't want to die, please, mister, Doc, don't kill me," Emmanuel begged and cried for his life.

Where Oliver's heart was torn from the sorrowful plea, Jack was merely pissed off. "Listen closely. You might have well just sentenced yourself, the doctor, and the other man we left to die. Chasing down your worthless ass has cost us time. I would fucking slit your throat right now if I didn't know the good doctor would try to stop me. So shut up, get on your feet, and we're going back to the cabin where I'm, for some reason in hell, going to save you," he growled as he grabbed the kid by the coat and pulled him as close to his face as he could and then shoved him back against Oliver.

Oliver helped Emmanuel up. "Let's get back. My head is splitting, and I'm so exhausted I could drop right here." There was no point in him lying about it. There was a good chance that he would die before Jack could do whatever he was going to do. He was silently making amends for his imminent death through prayers and hoped that the others would be saved.

Jack's anger paused for a moment at the doctor's honesty. To hell with this kid and the other man. Yes, he was trying to be better, but there were limits. Those had been met a while ago. Were it not for this doctor and whatever power he held over him, he'd have killed the others swiftly and burned the cabin down. He had a feeling that whatever happened after this if the doctor survived, would not be the last he'd see of him. Jack mounted up on Wraith and then helped the other two to mount after assuring Oliver that 'yes, his horse could carry all three of them just fine.'

They went much slower on the way back but as fast as they could. Oliver dismounted, then helped Emmanuel down, and then Jack dismounted. "Go stable your horse, and I'll get him in," Oliver offered.

Jack whistled, and the colossal beast walked that way. "He'll be fine. He'd never leave me to just wander. Let's get on with this." He opened the door and saw Clyde slumped back in a chair, pistol on the ground, and a large hole in the side of his head. "Well, I suppose that's one less to save," he muttered, almost immediately feeling those judging eyes on him again.

"Shit. Clyde. "Oliver said as he moved over to the man and shut his eyelids. He must have done this not long after they had left because the lids refused to close. Instead, he took his bandana out of his coat pocket and draped it over his face.

Emmanuel stood still in the doorway with a disturbed look on his face. This cabin, which had been so warm and cozy, was now a nightmarish scene. There was blood everywhere. Things were still strewn about from the first fight with Daniel. The smell in the air was a mix of human waste, blood, and other bodily fluids mixed with a sour and bitter scent. It was like spoiled milk and wet marshlands melded together. "You run again, and I swear to the devil himself I'll shoot you. Now sit your ass down, both of you, and let me work," Jack ordered before he looked for a bowl to mix things in and brought it to the table. He pulled out a few things from the shoulder bag at his side. A small pile of what looked like bones, the tiny vial of blood he'd gotten from the black wolf, then he began looking for something else. It was apparent the Englishman wasn't able to find whatever it was. "Son of a bitch!" he mumbled angrily.

"What is it? What are you looking for?" Oliver asked with a growing worry. Emmanuel squirmed uncomfortably next to him.

Jack didn't answer as he rooted in every pocket, pouch, and satchel. After a moment, he pressed his fists to the table and bowed his head in defeat. Sanguinem ex Pura, the most important ingredient, was missing. Where could he get that now? And what the hell happened to what he had? Think, think, think. Jack's head snapped up, and he stared at Oliver as an epiphany hit him. "Oliver, come here," he commanded quickly, pulling out his dagger.

Oliver gave him a wary look and continued to sit there. "Why?" he asked cautiously.

Jack sighed heavily and then came over, dragged him out of his chair, and pulled him to his side of the table. "I'm not going to kill you. That would sort of defeat the purpose of me trying to save you, wouldn't it?" he snapped the query at him before he held the man's arm over the bowl and made a large enough cut that some of the doctor's blood would spill in it. "If either of you is the praying type, I would start now," he suggested to them as he began mixing the ingredients. As he did so, he spoke softly and slowly added water from his canteen. When he was done mixing, he poured two small glasses of the awful liquid and gave one to Oliver and Emmanuel. "Drink up, boys," Jack said with a smile.

Despite their lives being on the line, Oliver and Emmanuel stared at the strange man with unbelieving looks. "You're kidding, right?" Emmanuel asked in disgust.

"Yes, you got me. I'm wasting all our time on a bloody joke," Jack said with deadpan humor. "I'm going to be honest, I don't know if this will work. Depends on if my hunch is right," he said, looking at the doctor pointedly, "but I know that if you don't drink it, you will die. I will not force you to drink it, of course, but if I were you, I would."

Oliver looked at Emmanuel and weighed the options. No, he didn't consider the options, as only one option existed. "Here's to hopefully living through this," the doctor cheered dryly before holding his breath and tossing back the supposed cure. The taste was even worse than he thought. He knew it would taste coppery and metallic. After all, it was blood, but whatever else had been put in it made it even worse. He had to put a hand to his mouth as his stomach tried to get rid of the disgusting stuff.

Jack moved behind them and gave both backs a rub and a pat. "Atta boys, not so bad now, is it?"

Emmanuel was coughing harshly but was keeping the liquid down. Oliver was finally recovering from almost throwing up, but now his head was spinning, and his entire body felt heavy. "What, what's happening?" he asked as he struggled to open his eyes.

"You're both probably going to pass out for a bit; sorry 'bout that. Though you two could probably do for a bit of rest. Don't worry, you'll be fine when you wake up. Better than fine, you'll be cured," Jack told Emmanuel and Oliver in a chipper voice, even though there was that caveat of if the cure works. Otherwise, he'd make sure they wouldn't meet an end like the others. Both men bobbed in their chairs and looked concerned despite Jack's assurances. He couldn't blame them, though, considering he hadn't shown himself to be the most empathetic of people. "You have my word. I'll look after you," he promised again. This time, however, the look on his face was sincere.

Emmanuel or Oliver didn't utter a word while falling asleep in their chairs. Once Jack was sure they were out, he moved each to a more comfortable lying down position. He checked them over to see how many boils they each had on them while he did so. Emmanuel had a handful of them on his back, but they weren't at the final stage yet. Oliver had far more on him. Jack was surprised that the doctor hadn't complained about pain earlier.

He hoped he hadn't been too late with the cure. In the meantime, they slept and let the concoction work. Jack went outside and brought the bodies of the wolf and deer into the bedroom. The cabin would be burned whenever they left this place if they all could leave this place. If not, then he at least could say he tried.

CHAPTER FIVE

~ V ~

RECOVERY

Oliver woke up to the morning sunrise and the smell of a fire. His head was pounding, and his eyesight was blurry as he attempted to sit up straight. That's when he realized that there was a coat draped over him and one under his head. Next to him was Emmanuel, who was still out. "Good morning, sunshine. How are you feeling?" The question came from the other side of the room. Oliver saw Jack leaning back in a chair with his feet on the table, calmly smoking a hand-rolled cigarette.

"Like I've been in a path of stampeding buffalo," Oliver answered with a groan as he stood to his feet. He was still a bit wobbly, and the pounding headache didn't help. "If I hadn't watched you mix the horrible medicine together, I would swear that you got me drunker than I've ever been," he whined as he moved to sit down at the table with Jack.

Jack chuckled as he sat his chair back down and leaned toward Oliver. "Regardless, I'd bet my last pound you've never been drunk a day in your life." He said with a coy smirk before he took another drag of his cigarette. Then, he offered it to Oliver to share if he wished.

"No thank you," he said and waved the offer away. "Now, why would you think that?" he asked, but he didn't sound offended by it.He stared at him for a few seconds with a far too-pleased look as he passed a cup of coffee to Oliver.

"Educated guess," he said with a wink. He waited until the doctor took a sip of his coffee and then asked in a cheeky tone, "A virgin, huh? Rather shocking, considering how attractive you are. Under normal circumstances, I would have tried to charm my way into your bed for the night just for those dimples alone."

Oliver looked surprised, incredulous, and offended, "What? No! I'm not. Why would you...? How could you...? I fancy the fairer gender. Not that it is any of your business." His voice was absolutely defensive.

"Sanguinem ex pura," Jack said as if it was the most obvious answer in the world. The confused look on Oliver's face was precious. "Easy there, my darling. No need to get your panties in a twist. I'm not judging, and you shouldn't be ashamed. Well, maybe a little ashamed about lying about whom you fancy, but hey, everyone lies now and then." It had been a hunch, but thankfully he'd been right. That extra touch of pureness he'd felt from the man gave him the gut feeling.

"Sangua. What is that supposed to mean?" Oliver asked heatedly. His cheeks were flushed a dazzling red now. "And I'm not lying!" he was falling for it, poking at him to get him to either admit it or deny it so that it was apparent he was lying. Oliver had been raised a very conservative Christian, and he tried to live by the morals he'd been taught by his parents and the church they went to when he was still young. However, that didn't mean he was overly fond of how he was raised. According to the church's teaching, his proclivities were an abomination in the eyes of God. Oliver was an obedient son; unfortunately, he believed what he was raised to believe. Which was why he didn't drink, and it was why he was still a virgin. He was not about to tell Jack that. It wasn't any of his business.

Jack gave him a wolfish grin before exiting the table and moving around to stand behind Oliver. He leaned down close enough to whisper in his ear, "I'll keep your secret, but know you are missing out." His breath ghosted over Oliver's lobe before he straightened and patted his shoulders. "Up and at 'em, Manny boy. We should pack up and get out of this cabin. Then, we'll burn it to the ground just to make sure this disease doesn't get out," Jack said as he gave the young man a few shakes to wake up. The kid apparently didn't feel the shakes, and he was all out of patience with him. He leaned down and gave him a couple of slaps on the face. "Hey, wake up. Otherwise, I will set it on fire with your ass still in it."

Emmanuel groaned and mumbled, but slowly he got himself up. The way he grabbed his head, it was apparent he also suffered from a headache. "Damn, smarts, doesn't it?" Manny asked as he wobbled up to his feet. "Did it work?" he asked another question.

"Do you feel any sort of raging murderous intent?" Jack asked in a smart-ass way while he gathered some of his things back in his satchel.

"Um, no. Though, if I could murder this headache, I probably would," Emmanuel declared as he picked up his hat.

"Then it worked." As he approached the boy, his face became more serious and less friendly. Emmanuel was taller, but Jack was more built and more intimidating. He grabbed the kid's coat and pressed it into his hands. "I would highly suggest should anything like this happen to you again. Don't run." His eyes were piercing like daggers. Jack could tell Emmanuel would take his suggestion to heart by how hard he swallowed and nodded his head.

As the threat drove home, they silently continued to gather their belongings. It didn't take them long to clear their things and themselves out of the cabin. Jack found some lantern oil and dumped it around the area, especially where fire would catch fastest. He lit another cigarette before he used the match to set one curtain on fire. It was a bit of a shame to see this place burn. It was cozy and more than big enough for one or two people. It wasn't as if he had ever stayed in one place for a long time. Once the flames began to lick the wood walls confidently, he turned and walked out onto the small porch. The world outside was blindingly bright from the snow dumped over the area last night.

Jack looked around for the other two men and saw them at the stable. Emmanuel gave Oliver a handshake, a horse packed and ready to go. Before the young man mounted up, he looked at Jack and nodded. Then he headed off. The warmth of the fire was getting hotter as he stood outside the open door. It felt good, honestly, especially with the cold that had settled in with the snow. Jack took another long drag of his cigarette, the smoke mixing with the fog of his breath, before walking to the stable to get his horse ready. "Was it something I said?"

"Hm?" Oliver questioned as he turned to the man. "Oh! Emmanuel. I suppose I should be polite and tell you no. He was just eager to get home, but the truth is yes, it is because of you." His words were harsh, but his tone was jovial.

Jack put a hand over his heart and feigned a pained

look. "I'm wounded. Here I thought he could be my next best friend."

Oliver gave a dimpled laugh as he opened the stable door for Jack and then followed him in. "Oh man," he said as he rubbed both hands down his face, "the relief of being able to laugh this morning is surreal. I don't think I've ever been more thankful to laugh in my entire life." He paused for a moment to look at Jack. His expression was one of humble gratitude. "Thank you, Jack. You might be an asshole, but, I know we wouldn't have made it without you. We'd have either all died in that cabin, or we'd have brought that plague back with us."

Wraith, now visible in the daylight, was a massive horse with a dark blood chestnut coat. He stood still as Jack saddled him up. "You're welcome."

The sound of leather took over the stable space as the doctor debated asking Jack the other questions he had. Curiosity got the better of him. "As a doctor, I have to ask. What exactly was that illness? It started with the wolf, right? I've never heard of any beast carrying a disease like that. It wasn't rabies. I don't know of any other plague affecting animals that can also affect people that quickly. Those boils, the way they popped, how deeply they seemed to be rooted in the skin, I just don't understand it. Plus, other than some major illnesses most of the time, animals and humans can't infect each other with their maladies." His voice trailed off before he asked more questions. They were there, though, waiting impatiently on the tip of his tongue.

Jack finished clinching his saddle before he leaned against the horse and looked at Oliver. "It doesn't have a name, and yes, it started with the wolf," he spoke slowly as he weighed each word before saying them. There was not much more that could be told to Oliver about it without earning a confused look. He'd taken care of the wolf, though that was not what it was, so there would be no chance for it to spread that plague again. "You're just going to have to trust me on this. You'll be happier not knowing all the details," he tried to persuade him to leave it alone.

However, Oliver did not give up trying to learn something new. "What if it comes back? Affects some other poor soul who may spread it to a larger group of people? I feel like I must learn what we dealt with and how to stop it." His duty was to ensure people stayed healthy, and the thought of this running rampant in a town was terrifying.

"It won't come back. You have my word on that." Only the "wolf" could start the plague, and he'd ensured it would stay dead.

"Oh, oh good. I have the word of a stranger I watched coldly kill a man and seemed more than ready to practically kill a child without a second thought. Yes, I feel so much better. Thank you," Oliver's voice oozed with sarcasm. "Not to mention your cure. Now that the terror of being close to the worst death I've ever seen is gone, I've been able to think back to what you were doing. It looked more like something you read about witches doing. Plus, you used my blood for it, which you weren't even sure would work, so I feel you owe me a little better explanation," he argued. "Who are you really? I suspect you've lied to us about that as well."

Jack sighed and leaned his forehead against Wraith's side. "One of those was mercy, and I wasn't really going to kill the kid unless there was no other choice." He picked his head back up to look Oliver square in the eyes again. They were unfairly blue and intensely looking at him. The feeling of being judged washed over him again, and he had to fight not to turn his head away. "Witches? Me? No, not at all. Besides, who cares what the cure was? It worked, and that's all that matters. And I wasn't lying. My name is Jack Townsend. I'm originally from England and travel the world."

He'd had about enough of this interrogation, so he mounted up. "I don't know what to tell you other than you're just going to have to trust me. Now I must get going. I'm sure you'll be eager to get home yourself." Jack felt a pang in his chest after he said that. Something about this man made him want to stay by his side, to protect him or, even stranger, to be protected by him, but he knew that was silly. He had to work alone. It was safer that way.

"Maybe it was mercy, but you sure as hell looked like you enjoyed it," Oliver pointed out accusingly. "I care what the cure was. I'm a doctor. I just put something in my body that I do not know what it was and what it did," he was curious and worried about the after-effects. If it worked on more than just this disease, apparently eradicated now, it might work with other conditions. A scrutinizing gaze stared at the rugged-looking man as he restated who he was. Oliver couldn't tell if he was lying, but he also couldn't tell if he was telling the truth.

Then, the man announced he had to leave, causing his curiosity and irritation to be swept aside by a feeling he didn't expect, sorrow. He believed firmly that this man was dangerous, not only in a bad-boy way but genuinely deadly. Yet the thought of him leaving and never seeing him again was loathsome. He tried to ignore it. He'd never felt such an attraction to any man before. Though Jack was very good-looking, it was a different sort of magnetism. He decided to chalk it up because Jack saved his life and suffered post-trauma from everything that had happened. "Right. I suppose I should try to catch up with Emmanuel," he would not get any secrets revealed by Jack, and he would have to accept it.

Jack waited until Oliver was mounted, and they were both ready to leave this horrible place and all its bloody memories. He moved Wraith up closer to his horse and reached a hand down for a shake. "Despite all that, it was a pleasure to meet you, Oliver. I hope life stays a little more dull for you from now on. Who knows? Maybe we'll run into each other again sometime."

Oliver was trying to think ahead about what he would do when he got home. It all felt rather boring, but boring was good. Boring meant no one died a torturous death. Boring was no mysterious stranger that knew how to cure a disease he'd never heard of before. Boring was also not having a man being so openly flirtatious with him. Did the man not realize how blasphemous that was, or did he just not care? Oliver took his hand and shook it firmly. "I owe you my life, Jack. You have my eternal gratitude for that. Take care of yourself. If you're ever in the area again, visit our growing town of Center City."

"I will keep that in mind should I ever decide to come back this way. Might not be for a very long time," Jack released his hand. Silence fell between them again, neither wanting to be the first to leave. Someone had to be first, so Jack took it upon himself to be the bad guy and turned away. "Goodbye, good doctor," he said with a wave, not turning around to look at him.

Oliver's breath caught in his throat as he wanted to tell him not to go. Thankfully, he stopped himself before saying, "Goodbye, Jack." He spurred his horse in the opposite direction, following the same trail Emmanuel had left. There were many glances backward to watch the giant horse and his rider until, finally, they were lost in the sea of trees. Oliver stopped looking back then, but his mind was still on Jack and everything that had happened. The curiosity was eating him alive, despite his rational mind telling himself that it would have to remain a mystery. That wasn't a satisfying feeling, but it wasn't like he could do anything about it now. Oliver picked up his chin and nudged his horse to go faster. He was determined to let it go and focus on catching up with Emmanuel and getting home.

CHAPTER SIX

~ VI ~

A PROPOSITION

Oliver and Emmanuel made it back to town. They decided it best not to tell the people the entire truth of what had happened to the other men that had come with them. Instead, they blamed the sudden blizzard and one wolf's attack on the deaths. A ceremony was held to remember the men since a funeral was impossible without the bodies. Once the dead had been laid to rest, metaphorically, life went on as usual. It felt like nothing had ever happened to them in the woods that night. Oliver tried speaking to the young man about it, but he was happy to let the memories fade into the past and never think of them again. He couldn't do that so easily, though.

It was a few months after the incident. Oliver had yet to get all of it out of his head. At night, he'd lie awake in bed and run over the events with as much detail as he could remember. A lot of those details involved Jack. He wondered what the man was doing now, where he was and was going. The horror of watching four men die in terrible ways had dulled in his mind and didn't disturb him as much. Jack, though, that asshole stayed as firmly in his mind as he had been while he was riding home.

Eventually, the thought he should have gone with him knocked around his skull until they stuck. The only thing that kept him from considering such a reckless idea was that the man did not seem like he ever wanted company. There was also the fact that he had no real reason to travel with him. He was a doctor, not an adventurer, and he had never been inclined to travel much. All the feelings he had about it were confusing and impractical.

Yet, still, he thought about it for all he tried every distraction possible to forget. Like today, exactly two months since he'd left that cabin and watched Jack disappear into the woods. He was in his doctor's office, waiting for anyone needing him to come in and ask for help. It was a slow day, though, which was good but only hammered in how bored the doctor felt. Cards were laid on his desk as he tried to pass the time with a solitaire game. Then there was a knock on the door, "Come in." The door creaked open to just a crack as a hand wrapped around the edge, and dark curly hair peeked in. A face followed that the doctor didn't think he'd see again.

"Did you miss me?" A familiar accented voice made of velvet and embers asked with a smirk.

Oliver could only stare in shock for a moment before standing up from his desk and before Jack. The impulse to hug him was ignored. "What the hell are you doing here? You said you wouldn't be back in this area for years."

No answer was given, but Jack felt it was easy for him to assume that Oliver had missed him. "That's one of the best benefits of going where you want, I can change my mind whenever I like." Jack was as free as the wind, so to speak, and he used that freedom to go where he wanted when he wanted. Money was not an issue for him, and as long as there was a way to travel somewhere, nothing could stop him. Oliver gestured for him to sit at his desk and then sat back in his chair. "How have you been since the last we met? Still, feeling alright? What about the kid?" he asked curiously.

Oliver's dimples were deep in his cheeks, a broad smile on his face. It was odd to be so happy to see this man whom he'd only known for a day, but they had gone through something traumatizing so that he could chalk up the feeling of attachment. "Other than wondering if all that had happened, I'm doing alright. It was hard to inform the families of their loved ones' deaths, but Emmanuel and I decided to not be fully honest about what had happened to them. He's doing okay, but he refuses to talk about it. I think he's trying to convince himself that it was a bad dream. He might do that, but I can't, so he's avoided me. In case I try to speak about it with him again," it bothered the doctor that he couldn't speak about it to someone.

"Seriously, though, other than being able to, why did you turn around and come back this way? You were heading in the complete opposite direction last I saw you."

Jack gave a chuckle and scratched his forehead. Leave it to Oliver not to let go of a question. He knew that much about the doctor at this point. To put it mildly, the events that had happened to him in the last two months had not been great. To explain it quickly, it was like Jack was an addict and fell off the wagon after leaving Oliver and the burning cabin. It had been years since the last time he'd made a mistake, and boy, did he ever make up for the time. Jack wasn't sure how to describe how it had happened. Still, it was like once he was alone again and didn't feel those virtuous eyes staring at him with judgment; there was no keeping himself in check.

Fighting his own nature was what he did daily. It was comparable to how recovered alcoholics had to keep themselves in check lest they fall into a bottle again. It only took two days before Jack realized he felt that old itch again. He fought it hard, and being alone made it easier, but then he'd come across a station wagon heading back east. Jack wished he could say he had lost control and didn't remember doing what he did, but that was a lie. He remembered everything he'd done, and worse than that, remembered how much he'd enjoyed it, reveled in it. After that, he was sure that whatever good he'd done with those affected by the black wolf's plague had been undone by what he'd done to those on the stagecoach.

The last time Jack had fallen off the wagon like this, it had taken him a long time to get back in the right direction. Jack didn't want to go through that again. A deep part of him, the natural part, wanted to abandon being sober altogether, but he'd be damned if he didn't fight it. Oliver hadn't been far from his mind since that one night. It was a long shot, but remembering how the doctor made him feel, he thought it was worth turning around and finding him again. The adventurer didn't want to tell the doctor the truth about himself, who he was, where he was from, or what he was doing. Jack figured he could keep the man in the dark or spin a story close enough to the truth.

He felt those piercing blues staring at him again and looked up to realize that he'd been silent in thought for longer than he was meant to be. "Sorry, I got lost in thought there for a moment. I am actually here to make a proposition to you," he explained and then saw the skeptical look on Oliver's face. "No, not a sexual proposition. Unless you want me to," the doctor shook his head no vehemently, to Jack's amusement, before he continued. "I was hoping to tempt you into traveling with me." Those glacier lake blues widened as his jaw dropped a bit.

"You, you want me to come with you? Why?" Oliver asked curiously. His heart was beating faster at the fact the thing he'd been wanting was now being offered to him.

"Yeah. I could use a man like you by my side. You

know, someone who can fix me up when I hurt myself. It happens more than you'd think, I promise. And, I don't know, I like you, and I'd like for you to travel with me," he held up a hand quickly, "again, that's not a sexual thing. Unless you want it to be."

"I-ah. I don't know what to say. My office is here. I've just settled in," Oliver explained as he looked around the doctor's office. It was his job to help heal as many people as he could. Traveling across the world would be a serious obstacle. Yet, he knew that was precisely what he wanted to do.

Jack leaned forward and looked deep into those angelic eyes. "When have you ever done something because you wanted to do it? Not because it was expected of you?"

Oliver laughed and shook his head as he was ready to argue, but then he thought about it. Yes, he had chosen to become a doctor. Still, that was partially done because his parents expected him to do something proper with his life. In fact, most of his life had been determined by them or by what they had taught him. He'd never done something for himself besides moving here to start a practice. A different and exciting proposition was given to him, and it was one his parents would never agree to. Then again, they weren't here to agree or disagree and last he checked; he was old enough to make his own decisions. "You know what, yes. Yes, I will travel with you. This might be the worst decision I've ever made, but at least it will have been my decision," he answered triumphantly.

Jack gave a happy clap of his hands. "Brilliant. I was hoping you'd accept. Otherwise, I might have had to kidnap you." He winked at him in jest before he stood up. "We can leave tomorrow, or however long you need to pack. I will get you a better horse than that tiny thing you were riding before. This will be fun. Or, at the very least, it will be interesting, that I can promise." Jack shook the doctor's hand. The two spoke plans for the rest of the day and then set those plans in motion. By the morning light, the two of them would set off, ready to face whatever might come their way on the road again.

ABOUT THE AUTHOR

Parker Jack Plumer was born in the small town of Seymour, Indiana. Yes, the one from the song. They live with their husband, their child, and three kitties. Currently, they work as a merchandiser while trying to write and publish. This is the first book they've published, and, like most writers, thinks it's a garbage fire. The publishing name, Trashcan Printing, is a shout-out to their high school days when they first began writing.